PUF

The Legend of SPUD MURPHY

Eoin Colfer was born and raised in Wexford in the south-east of Ireland. His first novel, Benny and Omar, was a bestseller in Ireland, and Artemis Fowl, the first book featuring the brilliant young anti-hero, was a worldwide bestseller. It won the WHSmith People's Choice Children's Book of the Year and the Children's Book of the Year at the British Book Awards, as well as being shortlisted for the Whitbread Children's Book of the Year and the Blue Peter Book Award.
Eoin lives in Ireland with his wife, two sons and an overactive imagination.

www.eoincolfer.com

EOIN COLFER

The Legend of SPUD MURPHY

Illustrated by Tony Ross

PUFFIN

Published by the Penguin Group
Penguin Books Ltd, 80 Strand, London WC2R 0RL, England
Penguin Group (USA) Inc., 375 Hudson Street, New York, New York 10014, USA
Penguin Group (Canada), 90 Eglinton Avenue East,
Suite 700, Toronto, Ontario, Canada M4P 2Y3
(a division of Pearson Penguin Canada Inc.)
Penguin Ireland, 25 St Stephen's Green, Dublin 2, Ireland
(a division of Penguin Books Ltd)
Penguin Group (Australia), 250 Camberwell Road, Camberwell,
Victoria 3124, Australia
(a division of Pearson Australia Group Pty Ltd)
Penguin Books India Pvt Ltd, 11 Community Centre, Panchsheel Park,
New Delhi – 110 017, India
Penguin Group (NZ), cnr Airborne and Rosedale Roads, Albany,
Auckland 1310, New Zealand
(a division of Pearson New Zealand Ltd)
Penguin Books (South Africa) (Pty) Ltd, 24 Sturdee Avenue,
Rosebank, Johannesburg 2196, South Africa

Penguin Books Ltd, Registered Offices: 80 Strand,
London WC2R 0RL, England

www.penguin.com

First published 2004
This edition published exclusively for Nestlé breakfast cereals 2006
1

Text copyright © Eoin Colfer, 2004
Illustrations copyright © Tony Ross, 2004
All rights reserved.

The moral right of the author and illustrator has been asserted

Set in Baskerville MT

Made and printed in England by Clays Ltd, St Ives plc

British Library Cataloguing in Publication Data
A CIP catalogue record for this book is available from the British Library

ISBN-13: 978–0–141–32164–6
ISBN 10: 0–141–32164–4

contents

CHAPTER 1

Ugly Frank

I've got four brothers. Imagine that. Five boys under eleven all living in the same house.

On wet summer days, our house gets very crowded. If we all bring two friends home, then there could be fifteen of us crammed into the house. At least eight will be roaring like lunatics, and the rest will be dying to go to the toilet. The flusher in our toilet snaps off about once every three months.

When my dad came home one day and found three sons and four strangers covered in warpaint, swinging on the bedroom curtains, he decided that something had to be done. It didn't help that the warpaint was stolen from Mum's make-up box.

'No more bringing friends home!' Dad declared after the warriors' parents had collected them.

'That's not fair,' said Marty, the biggest brother, mascara streaking his cheeks. 'That punishment really affects me because I'm popular, but Will's best friend is his Action Man.'

Will. That's me. I love that Action Man.

Donnie, Bert and HP started complaining too. But only because they're little brothers, and that's what little brothers do for a living. I know that technically I'm a little brother too, but I'm in the big brother half of the family.

Having one little brother is bad enough, but having three is too much punishment for one person. That's enough punishment for an entire housing estate. The trouble with little brothers is that they are never blamed for anything. All Donnie, Bert and HP have to do is bat their blue eyes and let their bottom lips wobble a bit and they are forgiven for everything.

Donnie, Bert and HP could stick an axe in my head and they'd still get off with ten minutes' no TV and a stern look. The only things that Marty and I ever agree on is that our three younger brothers are spoilt rotten.

'This house is a madhouse,' said Dad.

'And he's the chief lunatic,' I said, pointing to Marty.

'I'm not the one talking to dolls,' retorted Marty.

That hurt. 'Action Man is not a doll.'

'Quiet!' said Dad through gritted teeth. 'There must be something we can find for you to do during the holidays. Something to get you out of the house.'

'Not my babies,' said Mum, hugging the younger brother squad tightly. They gave her the full baby treatment – big baby eyes, gap-tooth smiles and HP even sucked his thumb. That kid has no shame.

'Maybe not those three. But Will and
Marty are nine and ten now. We can find
something for them. Something
educational.'

Marty and I groaned. Educational
hobbies are the worst kind. They're like
school during the holidays.

Marty tried to save us. 'Remember the last educational hobby? The art classes? I was sick for days.'

'That was your own fault,' said Mum.

'I only had a drink of water.'

'You are not supposed to drink the water that people use to wash their brushes.'

Dad was thinking. 'What about the library?' he said finally.

'What about it?' I said, trying to sound casual, but my stomach was churning.

'You both could join. Reading. It's perfect. How can you cause trouble reading a book?'

'And it's educational,' added Mum.

'Yes, of course, it's educational too,' Dad agreed.

'How is it educational?' I asked, terrified by the idea. 'I'd much rather be outside riding a horse than inside reading about one.'

My mother tousled my hair. 'Because, Will, sometimes the only horse you can ride is the one in your head.'

I had no idea what that meant.

'Don't make us join the library,' Marty begged. 'It's too dangerous.'

'Dangerous? How could a library be dangerous?' Dad asked.

'It's not the library,' Marty whispered. 'It's the librarian.'

'Mrs Murphy?' said Mum. 'She's a lovely old lady.'

The problem with grown-ups is that they only see what's on the outside. But kids know the real truth. People forget to be on their best behaviour around kids, because nobody believes a word we say. Every kid in our town knew about Mrs Murphy. She was one of those people that kids steer clear of. Like Miss White, the teacher with the evil eye, or old Ned Sawyer, the tramp with the dribbling dog.

'She's not a lovely old lady,' I said. 'She's a total nut.'

'Will! That's a terrible thing to say.'

'But she is, Mum. She hates kids and she used to be a tracker in the army. Tracking kids from enemy countries.'

'Now you're being ridiculous.'

'She has a spud
gun under her
desk,' added Marty.
'A gas-powered one
that takes an entire potato
in the barrel. She shoots kids with it if they
make a noise in the library. That's why we
call her Spud Murphy.'

My mother thought this was all very
funny. 'A spud gun! You'll say anything to
avoid reading a book.'

'It's true!' Marty shouted. 'Do you know Ugly Frank from number forty-seven?'

My mother tried to look stern. 'You shouldn't call poor Frank ugly.'

'Well, how do you think he got that way? Spud Murphy spudded him.'

Mum waved her hands as if two annoying birds were flapping around her ears.

'I've heard enough. You two are going to the library for the afternoon and that's it. We'll make some sandwiches.'

We stood in the kitchen glumly. Sandwiches wouldn't be much use against Spud Murphy and her gas-powered spud gun.

CHAPTER 2

Stay on the carpet

Of course the little brothers thought this was hilarious.

'Nice knowing you,' said Donnie, shaking my hand.

'Yeth,' said HP, the word whistling through the gap where his front teeth used to be. 'Nithe knowing you.'

Five years old and already a smart alec.

'Can I have your Walkman?' asked Bert, who was already wearing it.

I swatted them with my Action Man.

'Do you hear them, Mum? They're teasing us already.'

'Oh, they don't mean it,' said Mum. 'Do you, my little men?'

'No, Mummy.'

Mum gave them a jelly baby each. I thought my head would pop with the unfairness of it all.

'Now, Marty and Will, go upstairs and wash off the rest of my lipstick. We leave in ten minutes.'

There was no escape. We pleaded and whinged for ten minutes solid, but Mum was not giving an inch.

'The library will be good for you,' she said, belting us tightly into the back seats of the car. 'You might even learn something.'

As we drove away, we looked back towards the house. Donnie was at the bedroom window, enacting a little play for our benefit. He had scrawled the name

'Spud' across the front of his white T-shirt and was scolding a small figure standing on the window ledge. My heart jumped. It was Action Man. Donnie's scolding grew more and more furious, until eventually he picked up my unfortunate toy by the heels and began whacking him against the ledge.

'No,' I squealed. 'Stop the car. Donnie is killing Action Man.'

Mum laughed. 'Really, Will. Killing Action Man. You'll have to come up with something better than that.

Through the window I could see Bert and HP clapping wildly as Donnie took a bow.

Mum dropped us at the library on her way downtown.

'I'll pick you up on my way home, after I collect your dad from work.'

We nodded, both too scared to talk.

Mum pointed her fingers at us like two imaginary guns.

'Try not to get spudded, OK?'

She was joking, but we couldn't laugh. We couldn't even manage a smile. Mum would be sorry when she came back, and our faces had been blasted by soggy potatoes.

'Right, off you go, up the steps. I'll just stay here to make sure you go inside.'

I growled quietly. Our plan had been to hide around the back for a few hours. Mum was smarter than we thought.

We climbed the concrete steps to the library doors. I decided to go first because Marty told me to. You're probably wondering what we were so scared about. I bet you're thinking that we were a pair of gutless chickens who would have been better off at home sewing our names on to handkerchiefs. But that's because you think

libraries are happy colourful places, where
the librarians actually like children. That
may be what most of them are like, but this
one was different. It was a place where
serious men read serious books and nobody
was allowed to show even a glimmer of a

smile. A smile could get you thrown out, a titter could get you spudded. And if you laughed aloud, you were never seen again.

A little boy rushed out of the library straight into Marty. The boy had tears coming out of his eyes, and someone had obviously been dragging him along by the scarf.

He grabbed Marty's jumper. 'Don't go

in there,' he cried. 'For the love of God, don't do it. I was one day late with *Five Go to Smuggler's Top*. Just one day. And look what she did to me.'

And just like that, the boy was gone, trailing a wrinkled scarf behind him, with only a puddle of tears to prove that he had ever been there.

'Wait,' we cried after the fleeing figure. 'Tell us what Spud did to you.'

But it was no use. The boy had disappeared into the back of a dark car, and sped off to safety.

There was a porch outside the library. The porch's walls were covered with posters about things like book groups and art competitions. All very educational. We looked at the pictures on the posters anyway. Anything to put off going into the library itself and facing Spud Murphy. We stayed there until Mum came up the steps and knocked on the window.

We had no choice but to go inside. It was just as I feared. There was nothing in there but books. Books just waiting to jump off thc shelves and bore me silly. They seemed to watch me from their perches. I imagined them elbowing each other.

'Look,' they said. 'Two more kids having too much fun. We'll soon put a stop to that.'

The library seemed to go on forever.

Row after row of wooden bookshelves, bolted to the floor at the bottom and the ceiling at the top. Each row had a ladder with wheels on the upper end. Those ladders would have made great rides, but there was zero chance of children ever being allowed to actually have fun in here.

'What do you want?' said a voice from the other side of the library.

My heart speeded up at the very sound of that voice. It was like two pieces of rusted metal being rubbed together. I held my breath and looked across the huge room. An elderly woman was leaning on a massive wooden desk, her knuckles bigger than acorns. Her grey hair was tied back so tightly that her eyebrows were halfway up her forehead. She looked surprised and angry at the same time. It was Spud Murphy without a doubt.

'I said, what do you want?' she repeated, banging the desk with an ink stamp.

We walked across to her desk, clinging to each other like two frightened monkeys. There was a whole box full of ink stamps on the desk, and two more hooked into her belt like six-shooters.

Spud Murphy glared down from a
great height. She was big. Taller than my
dad, and wider than Mum and my two
aunties strapped together. Her arms were
skinny like a robot's and her eyes were like
two black beetles behind her glasses.

'Mum says we have to join the library,'
I said. A full sentence. Not bad under the
circumstances.

'That's all I need,' grumbled Spud.
'Two more urchins messing up my shelves.'
She took a pen and two cards from her
drawer.

'Name?'

'M-M-Mrs Murphy,' I stammered.

Spud sighed. 'Not my name, dummy.
Your names.'

'William and Martin Woodman!' I
shouted, like an army cadet.

We had surrendered our names, and
our address was next. I was a bit worried
about that. Now Spud knew where we
lived, and could track us down if we ever
forgot to return a book.

The librarian filled in the cards,
stamping them with the library crest.

'Pink cards,' she said, handing them to
us. 'Pink means junior. Pink means you
stay in the junior section of the library.'

Marty noticed that the toilets were in

the grown-up section.

'What if we have to … go.'

Spud threw the stamp back in the box, slamming the lid.

'Think ahead,' she said. 'Go before you get here.

Spud led us down long aisles of wooden flooring to the children's section. She wore woolly slippers on her feet that polished the planks as she glided.

'That,' she said, pointing a knobbly finger, 'is the children's section.'

The section was actually a single box shelf with four rows of books. On the ground before it was a small patch of worn carpet.

'Do not set foot off that carpet until you leave,' she warned. 'Whatever boyish idea enters your head, ignore it. Stay on the carpet, or there will be trouble.' She bent over almost double until her beetle eyes were level with my own. 'Is that understood?'

I nodded. It was understood. No doubt about it.

CHAPTER 3

The Test

On that first day on the carpet, Marty decided that we should test Spud. When Spud said there would be trouble if we stepped off the carpet, what exactly did she mean? Did trouble mean a strict talking to? Or did trouble mean being suspended by your fingernails over a pit of alligators?

'I need to know how much I can get away with,' said Marty, tying his jumper round his neck like a bib.

'I don't need to know,' I said, remembering the boy who had run past us in hysterics. 'I'll just sit here and pretend to read.'

'You are such a chicken,' said Marty. 'No wonder Action Man is your only friend. I, on the other hand, am an actual hero type. I am prepared to take risks.'

'Why did you tie your jumper to your chest?'

'Wait and see, chicken boy,' said Marty.

My big brother walked round the edge of the carpet, checking if Spud would spot him.

'She can't even see us,' he said. 'We can do whatever we want.'

I was starting to get worried.

Whenever a boy did something wrong, grown-ups tended to blame the entire family. 'What are you going to do?' I asked.

Marty smiled. 'The best way to mess with a librarian is to put things back in the wrong place.' He rubbed his hands gleefully. 'They hate that. It drives them nuts.' Marty was an expert on messing with librarians. There had been several notes home from the school library. 'So I'm just going to switch a few books for Mrs Spud Murphy. By the time she finds out, we'll be home watching cartoons.'

Marty lay on his stomach and wiggled out on to the wooden floor. He glided across the polished planks on a double layer of wool. We had to admit it. Marty was the master.

Like a crocodile swimming down the Nile, Marty slid to the nearest bookshelf with barely a sound. He climbed on to the bottom shelf, and perched there motionless. There was only one other person at this end of the library – a short man with grey hair and bushy eyebrows. Marty waited until he moved away before he began causing mischief.

One book at a time, he switched almost every single book in the section. He put mysteries with romance, adventure with bird-watching and gardening with model aeroplanes. Spud would be furious. To make matters worse, Marty intended swapping the reference sheets at the end of each shelf. These pages told the reader what kind of book was on that particular shelf. Marty reached up slowly and tore the sheet from the clip that held it.

Suddenly, a shadow fell across my brother. It was a big sharp shadow, and it belonged to a big sharp person. I turned to

look. It was Spud. She had appeared without a sound, like a ninja librarian.

Spud stood, slippered feet apart, with her hands hovering over the book stamps on her belt. Marty hadn't seen her, and was still holding the reference page. It was too late to warn him. There was nothing I could do.

Spud's left hand moved with lightning speed, grabbing the book stamp and throwing it in one smooth precise motion. It tumbled through the air so fast that it hissed. Marty turned just in time to see the block of wood and rubber heading in his direction. It was too late to move out of the way. All Marty could do was close his eyes and squeal like a kitten.

The rubber stamp snagged the reference page in Marty's hand, plucking it from his fingers and stamping it against the shelf. The force of the throw was so strong, that the page stayed there for several seconds after the stamp had fallen to the ground. Two words were stamped on the page in purple ink: DAMAGED GOODS.

'I knew it,' said Spud slowly. 'I can always tell a troublemaker. I took one look

at you Master Martin Woodman, and I
knew you'd be off that carpet before I was
back at my desk.'

'You set me up,' said Marty, surprised.

'That's right. I was waiting behind the
shelf. The jumper trick was good, but I've
tracked a lot sneakier than you in my day.'

Marty stood slowly, no sudden moves.

'I'm sorry, Spu– Mrs Murphy. I'll never leave the carpet again.'

Spud slid across the floor on her slippers. 'Too late for that. Since you're already off the carpet, you can fix the damage you've done.'

'But there are hundreds of books. I can't remember them all.'

Spud ran a finger along the shelf. 'Each book has a number. This section starts at number five hundred and sixty.' She plucked a book from the shelf. 'Here it is. I've started you off. You get these in order by the time your mother comes to pick you up, and maybe I won't have to tell her how you set off the fire extinguishers.'

Marty's mouth flapped. 'But … I didn't.'

Spud put her hands on her hips. 'I know you didn't, and I'm sure your mother will believe that. Unless of course you've been in trouble before.'

Marty thought about it for a moment, then began rearranging books as fast as he could. He knew when he'd met his match.

Two hours and fourteen paper cuts later, Marty was finished. He sat on the carpet sucking his fingers.

'That wasn't so bad,' he said on the way to the exit. 'I've had teachers meaner than her.'

Marty was actually getting cocky again.

'Marty! Don't you remember the rubber stamp? She nearly took your head off.'

'Yes. That was cool. She must practise for hours. Do you think she'll really say that I set off the fire extinguishers?'

'I don't care,' I said. 'I just want to get out of here.'

Marty had started to wander over

towards Spud. I couldn't believe it. Mum
was outside, waiting in the car. I could see
her through the swing doors. We were
almost safe, and Marty was going over to
the librarian's desk.

'Excuse me, Mrs Murphy.'

Spud's head swivelled slowly, like a
tank gun. Her eyes landed on Marty.

'Martin Woodman. Back for more. I
would have thought you'd keep well away
from me.'

'Just one question, Mrs Murphy. You wouldn't really say I set off the extinguishers, would you?'

Spud smiled back at Marty. Her teeth looked like a row of icicles.

'Oh, wouldn't I?'

'I don't think so. Throwing a stamp is one thing. That was cool by the way.'

'You liked that, did you Martin?'

'Sure did.'

Spud opened the box on her desk. 'I have a collection of stamps here. One came in last week you might like. It's in the shape of a pirate flag. A lot of the boys like me to stamp it on to their forearms, like a temporary tattoo.' She began to close the box. 'But maybe you're too young.'

Marty was already rolling up his sleeve. 'No. I'd love that. On my arm. Wait until the lads in the swimming pool see this.'

Spud selected a stamp, inking it on a blue pad.

'Are you sure, Martin? This won't wash off for days.'

'I'm sure. Stamp away.'

'Well, if you're sure.'

Spud's smile widened. 'OK then.
Keep still.' The librarian rolled the rubber
stamp across Marty's forearm. Across and
back, three times. When she removed the
stamp, we leaned in to examine the pirate
ship. Only it wasn't a pirate ship. It was a
short sentence of three words. The words
were: I LOVE BARBIE.

'Oops,' said Spud. 'Wrong stamp. Sorry about that.'

Marty couldn't speak. If anyone saw those words on his forearm, he'd be teased for all eternity.

'You boys had better hurry up,' said Spud, placing the stamp back in the box. 'One more thing. Any more of your little games and I get nasty. There are worse things in this desk than rubber stamps.'

We walked to the door. Marty held his arm in front of him as though it belonged to someone else.

Spud called to him as he opened the door. 'Oh, Martin,' she said, 'enjoy swimming.'

CHAPTER 4

A Good Book

For the next few visits, I sat on the carpet pretending to read. I sat there until I felt sure the pattern from that faded old carpet had transferred itself on to my bottom. Marty spent most of the time licking his forearm, but it was no use. The stamp didn't fade, and now he had a blue tongue too. Sometimes Mum arrived early to take us home and would catch me pretending to read.

'Now, there's a sight to make any

mother smile,' she said. 'I knew you would love reading if only you would give it a try.'

That was it. We were doomed. Three afternoons a week, Mum decided, we would spend two hours in the library.

So three times a week we pretended to read quietly. Sometimes we forgot to be quiet, and then Spud would pay the children's section a visit. I remember the first time it happened. We were arguing over who owned the air in our bedroom. I said that Marty owned the air on his side of the room, but he said that he owned the air at ground level. This meant that I would have to climb on to the top bunk just to breath.

Suddenly a familiar shadow fell across the carpet, making me shiver. Spud stood there, feet apart, belt weighed down with rubber stamps. Without saying a thing, she pulled out a large flashcard from her pocket. On the flashcard was written the word *Shhh*. We got the message.

We couldn't fight, we couldn't shout, we couldn't make loud bodily noises. All the things young boys live for. Oh the

boredom! My head felt like it would fall off and spin across the wooden floor. I tried everything to entertain myself. Watching movies in my head, following the pattern in my carpet prison, eating strips of paper from the books. But most of all, I just dreamed of freedom.

Then one day, something strange happened. I was pretending to read a book called *Finn McCool the Giant of Ireland*, when something caught my eye. It was the first sentence of the story.

Finn McCool, it said, was the biggest giant in Ireland.

There was something about that sentence. It was... interesting. I decided to read a bit more. I wouldn't read the whole book, no way. But maybe just another couple of sentences.

Finn had a problem, said the book. Angus MacTavish, the biggest giant in

Scotland, wanted to fight him.

Well, I couldn't stop now. Two giants fighting! Maybe I'd just see how that turned out. And so I read to the end of the page, and then I kept right on reading. Before I knew it, I was lost in the tale of Finn McCool and Angus MacTavish. There was adventure and magic and battles and clever plans. Mountains exploded and wizards slew goblins. Magic goats talked and princesses turned into swans. It was another world.

'Ready to go?' said a voice.

I looked up. It was Mum.

'What are you doing here?' I asked.

There were shopping bags in Mum's hands. 'What do you think I'm doing here? It's time to go.'

I hugged the book to my chest. 'But we just got here. It's only…'

I stopped talking, because I had

spotted the wall clock. It was five o'clock. I had been reading a book for almost two hours. I looked across at Marty. He was still reading! A book with a picture of a dragon on the cover. What was going on here?

'Come on now, your dad will be
waiting.'

To my complete amazement, I
realized that I didn't want to leave my
book behind. And neither did Marty.

'But Mum…'

'Yes, Marty?'

'I've not finished my book.'

'Neither have I.'

Mum put down the shopping bags,
and gave us both a big hug. Right out in
public. It's a good thing our friends didn't

hang out in libraries.

'Do you think Spu– eh … Mrs Murphy would let us bring them home?'

Mum picked up the bags. 'Of course. You have your cards, don't you?'

CHAPTER 5

off the carpet

For weeks, everything was wonderful. We had the time of our lives. Every new book opened the door to a new world. We floated down the great Mississippi river with Huckleberry Finn. Robin Hood taught us how to shoot a bow and arrow. We caught burglars with the Famous Five, and Stig of the Dump gave us fort-building tips.

Spud Murphy generally left us alone, so long as we returned our books on time and didn't make any noise on the carpet. A few times she had to show us the *Shhh* flashcard, but we never got up to any real mischief.

Until…

One Monday, we ran out of books to read. We had read everything twice, even the Nancy Drew mysteries. We sat on the carpet dreading the boredom that would soon set in. It wasn't fair.

Marty was so bored he was licking his forearm again, even though the Barbie stamp was long gone.

He stopped licking to complain. 'What are we going to do?' he moaned. 'I can't sit here for six hours a week with no books.'

'Me neither.'

'It's such a tragedy. The adventure section is right over there.'

'The *adult* adventure section. We only have pink cards, remember?'

'I know, but if one of us just had the guts to go over there. One book is all we need to get us through the afternoon.'

I covered my head with a book. 'No way. Don't even ask. I'm not listening.'

Marty crawled over to me. 'Oh come on. I can't go. Spud has her eye on me.'

'But what about the spud gun?'

Marty pinched my cheek. 'You're the cute one, if Spud catches you, she'll probably give you a lolly.'

'No, Marty,' I whispered in case Spud heard.

'I'll let you breath my air in the bedroom.'

'No.'

'I'll let you hang around with me and the boys.'

'I don't want to hang around with you.'

'I'll tell you where Action Man is
buried.'

I gasped. 'Action Man is buried?'

Marty knew he had me. 'Yes.
Somewhere in the garden. The big garden.

I'd say the worms are starting to nibble on him around now.'

What choice did I have? Action Man needed me, and I did really want something to read.

'OK, Marty,' I hissed. 'I'll go. But only today. If you want a book on Wednesday,

you'll have to go yourself.'

Marty patted me on the shoulder. 'That's fair,' he said. 'Now, off you go. I want something really exciting.'

I put one foot off the carpet, on to the wooden floor. It creaked like a bat squealing. In seconds, Spud skated around

the corner, her slippers gliding over the
polished planks.

Shhh, said her card.

'Sorry,' I whispered.

Spud's beetle eyes squinted at us
suspiciously, but she continued on to the
romance section.

'I knew you couldn't do it, chicken
boy,' said Marty. 'Not even when Action
Man is counting on you.'

I stuck my tongue out at Marty. I
wasn't beaten yet, not with Action Man
buried in the garden. I would show Marty
that I was no chicken boy. I stripped off

my shoes and socks and tried again. With utmost care I lowered my big toe on to the boards, like a mouse testing a trap. No creak. Just beautiful silence. This could work. There were no adults at this end of the library, so I only had Spud to worry about. I took one little step. Then one more.

Every boy knows that if you want to cross a floor silently, then stick close to the wall. I stuck so close that I could almost feel my shadow tickling my back. Inch by inch I made my way towards the adventure section. Every patch of skin on my body was sweating. It felt as though my teeth were sweating. What would Spud Murphy do if she caught me? Would I get the stamp, or the spud gun? Spud gun, I guessed. After all, Marty had already received the family warning.

A ladder blocked my way. A library

ladder with wheels on the top. I needed
this ladder to reach the adventure books.
Gently I wheeled it along the shelves
towards the adventure section. It didn't
squeak once. Spud kept her ladders well
oiled.

I could see the books now, just out of reach. I climbed the ladder slowly, waiting for the creak that would bring Spud running. One step, then two, then three. High enough to reach for a book. I made

myself as tall as I could. Stretching from the tip of my big toe to the point of my index finger. I took a book from the shelf and stuffed it down the back of my trousers. Success. All that remained was the return journey to the carpet.

The trip back was just as scary. I was sweating so much that I began to feel thirsty. The distance between me and the carpet seemed ten times longer than it had on the way over, and every tiny sound I made echoed around the high walls. But I couldn't stop now. If I did, Spud would surely catch me on her next round. Then I would be spudded for sure. So I took step after sweaty step until the ladder was back in its place, and I was safe on the carpet.

Marty pulled the book out of my trousers. 'Well done, Will. I didn't think you had it in you.'

'Now tell me,' I demanded. 'Where is

Action Man buried?'

Marty grinned. 'In the toy box, sucker, where he always is.'

My big brother had tricked me again, but I was too relieved to be angry.

We took a look at the book's cover. *Spies in Siberia* it said across the top in gold letters. Underneath there was a picture of a man skiing down a snowy mountain. Spud would be able to tell from a hundred metres that this was no kid's book. So Marty borrowed a cover from one of the children's books and folded it over *Spies in Siberia*.

I put my shoes and socks back on and then we read happily for the rest of the afternoon. Those spies had a fine time with their fast cars and parachutes and kissing every girl they met. I could have done without the kissing, but the rest was great. It was the first time I had ever been this close to Marty for any length of time

without an argument breaking out.

At four-thirty, Marty hid *Spies in Siberia* behind a row of Enid Blytons, and we settled back to wait for Mum. I have to admit that I was feeling very pleased with myself. I had outwitted the famous Spud Murphy. Her tracking skills had been no match for my brain. I was the King of the Library.

Or was I?

Suddenly Spud glided round the corner on her woolly slippers. She skidded to a stop before us, sniffing the air like one of those mean dogs skinheads own. Her eyebrows seemed even higher than usual.

'Something's not right,' she said in her rusted metal voice.

We smiled innocently. Like most boys, we did a great innocent smile.

Spud glared at us. 'Innocent smiles don't work on me, little men. Unless you

really are innocent. Which I doubt.'

I could feel my smile shrinking, like a banana being gobbled up from both ends. Stay calm, I told myself. Thirty minutes and Mum will be here to save us.

Spud skated around the library floor in large circles, looking for something out

of place. Her eyes flitted across the polished wood, like an eagle's searching for a mouse. Finally she came to the spot where I had started my journey. She skated past it.

Whew.

Then stopped and turned back.

Oh, no.

Something had caught Spud's eye. Something in the exact spot where I had stood. She bent low to the ground, and followed my path to the ladder.

'Coincidence,' whispered Marty, from the corner of his mouth. 'Don't worry.'

Spud placed one hand on the ladder, pushing it along the shelves. She stopped at the adventure section.

This couldn't be happening.

The librarian climbed to third step, and reached out one knobbly finger. The finger pointed to a space on the shelf.

'Aha,' she said.

I couldn't believe it. She must have some magical powers. I was in deep trouble. The deepest.

Spud climbed down and skated over to the carpet. She stopped before us and said three words.

'*Spies in Siberia*?'

I tried my innocent smile again. 'Pardon?'

'*Spies in Siberia*. One of you took it from the adventure section. Hand it over.'

By now I was too scared to speak actual words. I did manage to shake my head. No, the shake said, it wasn't me.

Marty did a bit better. 'I would never ignore library rules and leave the children's section,' he said, straight faced. 'That would be wrong and my parents would be so disappointed.'

Spud squinted at us through beetle eyes. 'So that's the way it is,' she said. 'OK, then, I want both of you to lie down.'

We obeyed, and with deft movements, she whipped off our shoes and socks. She studied our bare feet, and eventually settled on me.

'Stand up,' she ordered.

I did as I was told. Wouldn't you if Spud Murphy was looming over you?

Spud tucked her hands under my arms, lifting me fifteen centimetres straight up.

'I think it was you, William,' she said. 'Because you left a trail.'

What trail? I couldn't have left a trail.

Spud glided over to the wall where I had begun my journey, and set me down right on my own sweaty footprints. I had left a trail all right. A trail of dried footprints.

'Now,' she said sternly, 'hand over
Spies in Siberia.'

I was caught. Fair and square. The
evidence was against me. What could I do
but return the book and beg for mercy. I
trudged back to the children's section and
took my borrowed book from the shelves.

Marty shook his head in disgust.
'Shame on you,' he said. 'How
could you break library
rules?'

I ignored him, too busy wondering what terrible punishment Spud would inflict on me.

'Here,' I said, handing her *Spies in Siberia.*

Spud shook her head in wonder.

'Why did you do it? Aren't you terrified of me? All the other children are.'

At that moment, I made the best decision of the afternoon. I told the truth, or at least some of it.

'I wanted a book,' I said in a shaky

voice. 'I had read all the others, most of them twice. I had to get a book.'

'Even though you knew I might catch you?'

My bottom lip was wobbling like a red jelly worm. 'It was worth the risk.'

'Right!' said Spud. 'Stand in front of my desk. I have something for you. And it's not a rubber stamp.'

Oh no! The gas-powered spud gun. I was going to get spudded. Time to beg.

'But...'

Spud raised her hand. 'No buts. You're going to get what you deserve. Go on, in front of my desk.'

I walked to the desk, more frightened than I had ever been in my life. This was it, the end of my time as a cute kid. From today on I would be known as Weird Will, the Spud-face Kid. It was too much. I closed my eyes so I wouldn't see it coming.

My ears kept right on working, supplying noises for my imagination to add pictures to. Behind me, Marty was still making *tsk tsk* sounds of disgust, as though

I had let him down. In front of me I heard Spud rooting around in her desk drawer. She was probably loading the spud gun, picking a really hard potato.

'Open your eyes!' she ordered.

'No,' I moaned. 'I can't.'

'Come on, William Woodman. Look at what I've got for you!'

I took a deep breath and opened my eyes. Instead of the barrel of a spud gun, there was a blue card in front of my eyes. Behind the card was Spud's face. She was smiling and her teeth didn't remind me of icicles any more. They looked friendly.

'A blue library card,' she said. 'Blue means adult. Blue means you can go anywhere you want in the library. All I ask is that you show me any adult books you pick, so I can check if they're suitable for you.'

I was amazed. Could Spud be

rewarding me for breaking the rules?

'W-w-why?' I stammered.

Spud smiled again. It quite suited her face.

'Because you left the carpet for a book. Not to cause mischief. Books are what this library is for, sometimes even I forget that.'

Wow. I had done something good, by accident. Wait till Mum heard about this.

Spud winked at me. 'Maybe it's time I expanded the children's section, and got rid of that carpet.'

I thought about it. 'Maybe you could leave the carpet where it is. But just as somewhere to sit.'

Spud put out her hand. 'It's a deal.'

I shook her bony hand. Winking and hand shaking? Maybe aliens had abducted the librarian and left this Spud-shaped robot in her place.

'Mrs Murphy, seeing as we're so

friendly now, would it be OK if I called you Spud?'

The librarian put her free hand under the desk. She twisted something, and whatever she had under there began to hiss gently.

'Just try it once, Woodman, and see what happens.'

I backed away slowly.

'Maybe I'll just wait for Mum on the carpet.'

'Good idea.'

Now, I know what you're thinking. Surely after Marty's terrible behaviour I would stay well out of his reach. Well, you're nearly right. I did stay out of his reach, about fifteen centimetres out of his reach. I stood a metre off the carpet and waved the blue adult card at him.

'Get me a book,' he begged.

'After that Action Man trick you pulled? Forget it.'

'Come on. You can breathe the bedroom air.'

'Well, OK,' I said, and brought him *Roses in Autumn* from the romance section.

'Not this one,' he cried, reading the back cover. 'I don't want a book about someone called Penelope.'

I was already halfway up the adventure section. I cupped one hand round my ear as though I couldn't hear him, and he didn't dare shout. When I glanced Marty's way, a few minutes later, he was twenty pages into the romantic novel.

At ten past four, a horn beeped three times outside. One long beep, two short beeps. Our signal. Mum was waiting. We quickly chose a book to take home. Marty was borrowing *Roses in Autumn*.

'There's a lot of sword fighting,' he said as Spud stamped the book.

Spud stamped my book too. Slipping my blue library card into a little envelope.

'You know, Will, now that we're so friendly, maybe you could call me Angela?'

I tucked my book under one arm.

'See you Wednesday, Angela,' I said.

Spud smiled. 'See you Wednesday, Will.'

And she did.